Dear Wally,

I've got this problem. . .

Dear Wally,

I've Got This Problem . . .

by Wally the Turtle
with a little help from
Mary Lou Carney

Fleming H. Revell Company
Tarrytown, New York

Illustrations by Susan Scruggs and Charles Cox
Cover illustration by Stephen DeStefano
Book development by March Media, Inc.

Copyright © 1991 by Mary Lou Carney
Published by Fleming H. Revell Company
Tarrytown, New York 10591
Printed in the United States of America

START HERE

Hi, kids! And welcome to my book—well, it's really not *my* book. It's *your* book, full of lots of the letters you've written to me. There's the letter from Tristan, who has to go to a new school next year. And a letter from Alex, whose family is always yelling at one another. Robin wrote for some advice on how to make friends. Odette wants to know how to get her mom to stop smoking.

Kids from all over write to me, and every single letter has one thing in common—a kid with a problem. So if you've got problems, that makes you *normal*.

Here in the letters in this book you'll find answers—how to survive wearing braces, how to handle playground bullies, how to get better grades on tests, how to deal with the death of someone you love.

But you'll find some fun stuff too. (Did you know the first *sun*glasses had nothing to do with sun? Or that American homes have more TV sets than bathtubs, refrigerators, or toilets?)

You'll also find out that you don't have to deal with your problems alone. Lots of people are willing to help you. Most important of all, God is on your side—no matter what!

So come read my mail—and meet fifty-two kids a lot like you.

WALLY

Dear Wally,
    I'm having a problem with a girl named Summer. She thinks it's wrong for me to have other friends. This really bugs me! Help!

                    Heidi

You can have a lot of friends at the same time. When it comes to friends, more can be better!

Dear Heidi,

One of the reasons Specs and I are such good friends is because we each have so many other friends! Having a friend who wants to control all your time isn't much fun! Did you ever wonder why Summer is like that? Maybe it's because she feels unsure of herself. And that puts you in a tough spot, because people who are insecure often cling too tightly to their friends.

If you really want to be friends with Summer, you'll have to make her understand two things. The first one is that she is important to you. Why not do something special with just her once in a while—see a movie, sleep over, go to the mall? The second thing she must realize is that you want to have other friends. Tell her this gently but firmly. And try to get Summer to "be interested in others, too, and in what they are doing" (Philippians 2:4, TLB). Then you and Summer—and all your friends—can have a great time together!

WALLY

FUN FACT

American homes have more TV sets than bathtubs, refrigerators, or toilets.

Dear Wally,
   I like to watch scary shows on TV, and I know they are not good for me. What should I do? They give me nightmares.

Travis

Psychologists say if you watch a lot of horror movies, you're much more likely to be less concerned when real people are hurting. You may not be able to care as much.

Dear Travis,

Have you ever eaten worms—big, slimy, gooey worms? Let's pretend you did and they made you sick. Would you eat them again? Of course not! You'd be too smart to do something when you knew it would make you feel bad. So if you won't put garbage into your stomach, why do you want to put it into your mind?

God doesn't want us to be afraid. "So do not fear, for I [God] am with you....I will strengthen you and help you" (Isaiah 41:10, NIV). But God expects us to use the good sense He gave us to stay away from frightening situations whenever possible.

Sounds like you already know the answer to your problem. "I know they are not good for me....They give me nightmares." Then why do you watch them? Instead, why not read a riddle book or work a puzzle? You could call a friend or bake cookies with your mom, go to the mall or ride your bike, write a poem or climb a tree. There's lots of things to do besides watch TV!

The next time you see a scary movie coming on, hit the OFF button and move on to something else. You'll be glad you did!

WALLY

ARE YOU SCARED TO ADMIT YOU'RE SCARED?

Well, don't be! Just keep in mind that . . .

- Everybody's afraid of something. Everybody. It may be spiders or bullies or bad dreams. The world is full of things that can frighten people. Being scared makes you—normal!

- Talking can take away some of the terror. Find someone you feel comfortable with and tell him (or her) what scares you. Don't worry about sounding silly. Talking will help you understand exactly what you're afraid of. And you may even find out how someone else has overcome a fear a lot like yours.

- God will help. Have you ever wished for someone big enough to take care of whatever scares you? There is someone like that, someone with more power than all the super-heroes rolled into one— God. Nothing is too big—or too small—for Him. Why not talk to Him right now about whatever scares you?

Dear Wally,

I have a problem about next year. The kids in Bellevue Heights subdivision where I live will have to go to a different school. I've been worried about it for three days. I'm shy when I go to other schools and see other people. Sometimes I'm scared. What can I do to not be scared and not be shy?

Your friend,

Tristan

"I have to go to a different school. What can I do not to be scared and not be shy?"

Dear Tristan,

Going to a new school can be scary, but it can be exciting too! You could have a super-cool teacher, or find a friend who likes all the same things you do. Maybe you'll be the fastest runner in your gym class, or win at spelldowns.

It's only normal to feel shy around people you don't know. So the solution to your problem is . . . get to know them! Let the kids at your new school see that you're friendly. Smile. Talk. Share yourself! Treat your new friends the way you'd like to be treated. And don't feel you have to pick a best friend right away. Take your time! Make lots of new friends.

But the best thing is that, whatever school you attend, God will go with you. He says so right in the Bible: "Do not be terrified; do not be discouraged, for the Lord your God will be with you wherever you go" (Joshua 1:9, NIV).

It's going to be a great year, Tristan!

WALLY

Dear Wally,

I have this problem about my sister. I do not know what to do. See, she is 15 and she has gone to live with my father. I really miss her. What should I do? Write, call, what?

Jayne

Dear Jayne,

Have you ever heard that old expression, "You don't know what you've got till it's gone"? Sometimes it's true. We don't realize just how much our friends—and family—mean to us until they're not around all the time.

You didn't tell me whether your sister's moved across town or across the country, but—either place—writing a letter is a great idea. Everyone loves getting mail (even turtles!). And a letter can be read again and again. Tell her what you're doing. Add a stick of her favorite gum. Recall the fun times the two of you have had. Show an interest in what she's doing by asking questions about her new school or neighborhood.

If it's not long distance, or if your mother will let you, call her some Saturday morning and catch up on all the news. Visits, of course, would be great—maybe during school breaks or summers.

Why not make your sister little mailable surprises? Cut out a fancy paper snowflake to remind her of the time the two of you went sledding. Draw a cartoon of something funny that happened at your school Or you could even bake her a shoebox full of her favorite cookies.

But it's important that you don't spend all your time thinking about your sister and how much you miss her. "Even in laughter the heart may ache" (Proverbs 14:13, NIV). Life has to go on. Try some new activities on your own. Join a club at school, get involved in your church, start a new hobby. How about keeping a diary?

You can make new friends without losing the special bond you have with your sister. And if you work at staying in touch, the two of you can still be close—whether you're in the same room or just in the same hemisphere!

Wally

Dear Wally,
    I have a problem with my family. We are always yelling at each other. I want my family to be a lot nicer. I hope you can help me.

alex

Dear Alex,

When you visit a friend, or even a faraway relative, did you ever notice how you put on your best behavior? You try to remember to say "thank you" and "please." You don't grab for the best toy or the biggest piece of pizza. You'd never dream of acting rude. But with your own family . . .well, it's a different matter.

When people live together day after day, they begin to take each other—and each other's rights—for granted. Maybe your little brother trashes your room, or your sister borrows your clothes without asking. Your mom has a bad day at work; Dad is tired. Tempers flare and words fly.

There's no easy answer to your problem, Alex. Ask for a family meeting and talk together about what each of you can do to make things better. Make a list of everyone's suggestions. Then post it in an important place (maybe on the refrigerator door).

But the best advice of all is God's. "Treat others as you want them to treat you" (Luke 6:31, TLB). Why don't you—and your family—try it? It works!

WALLY

Dear Wally,

I have a problem. I'm fat and ugly. The other kids always call me names. I probably will never get a girl-friend. Also, I'm not good at all at sports. Everybody can kick a ball farther than me, even some of the girls. Please help me with my problems.

Tyler

Ugly doesn't have to do with how big your nose is or how curly your hair is. It has to do with meanness on the inside.

Dear Tyler,

Who says you're ugly? The people who are really important in your life—or a bunch of guys who want to make you mad? Believe me, Tyler, you are not ugly. How can you be when you were "created . . .in the image of God" (Genesis 1:27, NIV)? Ugly doesn't have to do with how big your nose is or how curly your hair is. It has to do with meanness on the inside. And it sounds to me like the kids teasing you may be the ugly ones!

You say you're not good at sports. Lots of people (and lots of turtles!) aren't. Find out what you can do well. Maybe it's math or stamp collecting. If sports are important to you, practice. Nobody ever gets better by not trying. Eventually you'll get better, not great maybe, but definitely better! Who knows—the exercise may help you get rid of some of your extra weight, too.

And as for the girlfriend, once you start liking yourself more, you may be surprised who else will like you too!

WALLY

Dear Wally,
    I have a question to ask. When you die, do you become a baby animal or a tree? I have lots of dreams about this.

                    Your friend,
                    Aaron

Dear Aaron,

When I'm curled up snug inside my shell, I have the most interesting dreams. Sometimes they're funny and weird. Sometimes they're exciting. And sometimes they're scary. Psychologists tell us that dreams are the way our minds sort through what we've been wishing for or worrying about. They aren't real, and they don't often come true.

Have you ever sat in your room and listened to the noises in your house? A squeak here, a thump there? The sound of a voice or a radio? And no matter how closely you listen, it's impossible to know exactly what's happening outside the walls of your room. Those walls keep you from seeing beyond where you are.

Death is like that too. An invisible kind of wall separates life and death. We can't know all about what it's like to be dead. That's why so many weird and frightening stories are made up about it. But some things we know for sure about death. Things the Bible tells us. Death is a change from a body that can get bad colds and broken arms to a spirit that will live forever. When you die, your soul does not go into the nearest pine tree or porcupine. It goes to be with God. "And it is appointed unto men once to die, but after this the judgment" (Hebrews 9:27, KJV).

So when you hear stories about people coming back as baby animals or plants, realize that they're just that—stories. And soon you may find yourself thinking—and dreaming—about lots of fun stuff.

WALLY

Dear Wally,
  I don't like onions, but my mom puts them in the food. What can I do?

  Christian

Dear Christian,

I love onions! I even put them on my ice cream sundaes! They're so crunchy and spicy and . . . .

But it's clear that you dislike onions as much as I like them. And it sounds like your mother is a real onion fan—putting them in lots of the food she makes.

Every issue has two sides, Christian. The Bible says you should "look not only to your own interests, but also to the interests of others" (Philippians 2:4, NIV). Your mother does all the cooking, and I'm sure she wants her recipes to turn out the way they are supposed to. You, on the other hand, feel you have a right to food without something you hate—recipe or no recipe.

Maybe you and your mom could compromise. You could learn to eat onions in a few things like meatloaf and chili. And your mom would promise to never put them in certain other things like pizza or spaghetti.

No one gets his way all the time, but talk this problem over with your mom and suggest that a few days each week feature "onion-free" cooking. And don't forget to compliment her on how yummy everything tastes!

WALLY

Dear Wally,

My sister has learning disabilities and has to go to a special school. But this boy in my school makes fun of her, and even though she's not there, I am—and I don't like it one bit!!! I love her a lot, and I'd hate to see her get hurt. Sometimes he's even mean to me. But sometimes he can be a friend! What should I do?

Courtney

It's easy to look at famous people and think they've got it all—intelligence, looks, money. It's easy to forget that many of them struggled with some of the same things kids today face, things like learning disabilities.

Take Thomas Edison for instance. A real genius, right? But he did poorly in school—so poorly, in fact, that the teacher expelled him, saying he was too retarded to ever learn! But it wasn't Edison's intelligence that kept him from doing well in class. It was his learning disability.

Former Olympic gold medal winner Greg Louganis remembers his school days. "I honestly thought I was retarded, because diving was the only thing I could do well." It wasn't until he enrolled at the University of Miami that Greg found out he was dyslexic. Dyslexia is a kind of learning disability that makes it difficult to read and learn.

And even though dyslexia can't be cured, it can be overcome. Just ask former Olympic decathlon star Bruce Jenner, or Tom Cruise, who says he made up for his dyslexia by becoming a good actor.

Learning disabilities are nothing to be ashamed of—or to make fun of. Like freckles or pug noses or curly hair, they're just part of what makes some kids unique.

Dear Courtney,

People make fun of what they don't understand. And lots of people don't understand about learning disabilities (LD).

They don't know, for example, that one out of every ten Americans has a learning disability. Or that most of these people have average or above-average intelligence. Some of them are even geniuses! A learning disability simply means that there is a difference between a person's intelligence and the way he or she performs in school. Kids with learning disabilities may learn in different ways from their classmates. But many LD kids are smarter than the kids who make fun of them!

Maybe telling this boy the facts will help. He doesn't seem all bad, since "sometimes he can be a friend." Take advantage of one of those friendly moments to explain your sister's problem to him. Remind him that all of us have things we'd like to change about ourselves. And since nobody's perfect, it's best to "never criticize or condemn—or it will all come back on you. Go easy on others; then they will do the same for you" (Luke 6:37, TLB).

Sometimes people try to make themselves seem smarter or better by tearing down someone else. But it doesn't work that way. The people who stand tallest are the ones who bend down to help someone else. That's a lesson this boy—and lots of others—need to learn. And you're doing a good job of showing them, by example, just how that works. Let's hope they're quick learners!

WALLY

Dear Wally,

I have a lot of trouble finding and making friends. Right now I only have one friend and am trying to make more. I don't think I'm mean. But I never ask anybody if they want to play or if I can play. Can you give me any ideas about making friends?

Robin

"A man that hath friends must show himself friendly..." (Proverbs 18:24, KJV).

Dear Robin,
   Yes! I *can* give you some ideas about making friends.

HOW TO MAKE A FRIEND

◆ *Don't be shy.* Sometimes people think you are a snob when you're only shy. So even if it's hard for you to make friends, let others know that you're friendly. Make the first move!

◆ *Treat your new friend the way you want to be treated.* Would you like to have the biggest piece of cake or be the first in line for the high dive? Let your friend! Not only will she like being treated so special, she'll probably start treating you the same way. If you want to have friends, learn how to be a friend.

WALLY

Dear Wally,

   I had to get a retainer about two years ago. It was to straighten my teeth and it was removable. That was the only good thing about it. Now I've got to get one again! But there's no good thing about it. This one isn't removable! It's like braces. No gum, caramel, raw carrot sticks, peanuts, popcorn or even JUJUFRUITS. Can you help me?

Lauren

P.S. I'll probably starve. I love gum!

FUN FACT

A primitive form of braces was used as far back as ancient Egypt. Today, over 4 million people are involved in orthodontic treatment. If you're one of them, grin! The future looks bright for your pearly whites!

Dear Lauren,

Wearing a retainer all the time can be a drag, especially when you have to give up eating your favorite foods. How long do you have to wear it? Six months? Two years? Any amount of time seems like a long time to you now, but think what a little chunk it is compared to the rest of your life. And that's how long you'll be able to enjoy your straight, healthy teeth! "There is a right time for everything..." (Ecclesiastes 3:1, TLB), and now's the time to straighten those teeth!

Will you do me a favor, Lauren? Spend the next ten minutes thinking about all the good stuff you *can* eat (with your dentist's approval): ice cream and frozen yogurt, pudding and Popsicles, bananas and peanut butter and whipped cream. . . . You still have lots to smile about!

WALLY

Dear Wally,
    I know this girl who doesn't know or love Jesus. She also uses His name in vain. When I tell her to stop, she keeps going. What should I do?

Donna

Do you know what the strongest muscle in the body is? The tongue! It's also the hardest one to control. If you sometimes find yourself saying things you wish you didn't, this prayer can help: "May the words of my mouth . . . be pleasing in your sight, O Lord" (Psalm 19:14, NIV).

Dear Donna,

Perhaps if you knew why this girl uses Jesus' name the way she does, you could help her change her behavior. But it is . behavior. If she chooses to keep on the way she is, it's her choice. And you must choose whether or not you want to be around someone who does something you know is wrong.

The Ten Commandments tell us, "You shall not use the name of . . . God irreverently . . . You will not escape punishment if you do" (Exodus 20:7, TLB).

So be friendly, but firm. Let her know that although you like her, you don't like what she's doing. And pray for her. If she "knew and loved Jesus," she wouldn't want to hurt Him by using His name in a disrespectful way.

WALLY

Dear Wally,

My mom has divorced and the divorce is final next Friday. My mom is going to start dating other people. And I want her to get married to my dad again. Can you help me?

Roy

Dear Roy,

Divorce can be a really rotten thing. And kids are usually caught in the middle because they love both parents. I'm sorry it had to happen to you, Roy, but you need to face the facts. Chances are your mom and dad won't ever marry each other again. And even though they are starting separate new lives, they still love you lots—and they need your love now more than ever. The kind of love that "does not demand its own way" (1 Corinthians 13:5, TLB).

Why not think of some ways to show them you still love them? Maybe a special picture for your mom, a letter to your dad? How about serving breakfast in bed or writing a special poem? Whatever you decide, you'll find that just doing something for someone else will make you feel better!

WALLY

NOTHING LASTS FOREVER— NOT EVEN:

- rainy days
- bad colds
- skinned knees

AND NEITHER DO THOSE FEELINGS KIDS GET AFTER THEIR PARENTS DIVORCE:

- sadness
- anger
- confusion

TIME AND TALKING ABOUT THOSE FEELINGS CAN HELP. SO CAN KNOWING THAT:

- kids are not to blame for the divorce.

Dear Wally,

I have to get glasses in a few months. I'm afraid that my friends will make fun of me. I mean, when my friend got a haircut everyone made fun of her. Just imagine what they're going to say to me! Can you help me?

Cara

FUN FACT

Eyeglasses have been around for almost 700 years. Today, 134 million people in the United States wear glasses. That's over half the population!

Dear Cara,

Okay, let's imagine what they're going to say to you. They might call you "four-eyes" or "glasses face." But they might say, "Cute glasses!" or "Now that you can see to hit the ball, play on my team."

One thing is for sure—your classmates will notice, just like they noticed your friend's haircut. Anything new is always material for teasing or comment. But nothing stays new for long, and people usually get tired of teasing if it doesn't get much of a reaction.

So stop expecting the worst! Your glasses may make your eyes look bigger and prettier. (You should see how weird Specs looks without his!) Not only will your glasses make the world look better to you—they may make you look better to the world!

WALLY

35

Dear Wally,

I have a problem in math. My teacher says I'm doing OK, but now we are doing division. I am not very good at division. Some of my friends say use a calculator. Some say do not cheat, just work at it and you will get there. Most of them say take the hard way out. What should I do, Wally? I'm confused.

Larry

Dear Larry,

Sounds like most of your friends are already giving you some good advice! Calculators are great little creatures. (I use one to help me keep track of my birthdays!) They make figuring out math answers so easy. And doing it on your own can be so hard. But calculators are meant to be used as tools. They can help you do quickly things you already know how to do. They'll let you check your work. And they can be your best friend when you get to really advanced calculations.

But if you don't learn the basics—like division—then the calculator becomes a crutch. You won't be able to figure out anything without it. So even though it's tough—do the work. "Study to shew thyself approved unto God" (2 Timothy 2:15, KJV). Your brain will last you a lot longer than any batteries will!

WALLY

ARITHMETIC

Arithmetic is where numbers fly like pigeons in and out
of your head.
Arithmetic tells you how many you lose or win if you
know how many you had before you lost or won.
Arithmetic is numbers you squeeze from your head to
your hand to your pencil to your paper till you get the
answer.
Arithmetic is where the answer is right and everything
is nice and you can look out of the window and see the
blue sky—or the answer is wrong and you have to start
all over and try again and see how it comes out this
time.
Arithmetic is where you have to multiply—and you
carry the multiplication table in your head and hope
you won't lose it.
If you ask your mother for one fried egg for breakfast
and she gives you two fried eggs and you eat both of
them, who is better in arithmetic, you or your mother?

Carl Sandburg

Dear Wally,

My mom smokes. When I tell her she could get lung cancer she says, "Shut up" and "If you keep nagging me I won't quit." My grandparents also smoke. They say, "It's a free world" and "The choice is ours. If we want to smoke, we can."

What should I do? I don't think I can stay around them much longer. Every time my mom smokes I start coughing, and she tells me to go to another room. I don't think that's fair. It's my house too. It's the same with my grandparents. Help!

Odette

If the effects of smoking appeared on the outside —instead of the inside, where it can't be seen—no one would smoke. No one would want to look that ugly!

Dear Odette,

It's hard when, day after day, you have to watch people you love hurting themselves. And smoking is just that—a way people have of hurting themselves. People smoke for all kinds of reasons. Some kids start because they want to look older. Or they think it's cool to break the rules at school or at home. But most adults—like your mom and grandparents—smoke because it is a habit. And 90% of these smokers want to stop. So why don't they? Some are afraid to try. Some have tried and failed. Some worry about gaining weight or being grumpy. Others simply don't know how to start to stop. The Bible says you should "honor God with your body" (1 Corinthians 6:20, NIV). And smoking doesn't do that!

It sounds like you've let your family know how you feel about their smoking. And that's good. But love can sometimes accomplish what scolding and complaining can't. Something as simple as saying, "I wish you didn't smoke because I love you and want you to live" can often make the smoker think about quitting. Why not try it?

WALLY

LET'S COUGH UP THE FACTS . . .

✗ Smoking is responsible for 87% of lung cancer.

✗ Cigarette smoking is addictive. The more you smoke, the more you want.

✗ Almost 1/3 of all cancer deaths are related to the use of tobacco.

✗ Cigarette smoke contains about 4,000 chemicals. Many are poison.

Dear Wally,

I have this problem. You see, boys don't like me. My parents always tell me I'm pretty. I think I should believe them. But when I get to school everyday and a boy comes up to me and tells me that I am ugly, it is really hard to believe my parents. What should I do? And can you give me some pointers on how to get boys to like me?

Cindy

Dear Cindy,

This boy at school—is he an expert on beauty? Does he have a special talent for sniffing out ugliness? Or is he just an ordinary boy who likes to tease girls?

There's more to being pretty than having long lashes and thick hair and straight teeth. The important people in your life will realize that. Have you ever heard that beauty is only skin deep? Well, real beauty goes much deeper than that. "Don't be concerned about the outward beauty that depends on jewelry, or beautiful clothes, or hair arrangement. Be beautiful inside, in your hearts, with the lasting charm of a gentle and quiet spirit which is so precious to God" (1 Peter 3:3-4, TLB).

Don't base your opinion of yourself on what others say about you. Not the kids at school or even your parents. You decide that you're attractive, worthwhile, important. God feels that way about you—so why shouldn't you feel that way about yourself? Then you don't overreact to compliments or "put-downs." And people like people who like themselves!

Who knows, if this certain boy can't get your attention with his "ugly" routine, he may try something else. Like a smile, maybe even a compliment.

WALLY

THE BEST KID ANYWHERE

I wish that I were pretty.
I wish that I were smart.
I wish that I were witty.
I wish with all my heart
That I could play the cello
And run Olympic sprints
Or be so very wealthy
I'd never carry cents.

I wish that I could yodel
And parachute from planes.
I wish I were a surgeon
Who could operate on brains
And make my patients smarter
Than they ever dreamed they'd be
So they'd know math and science
And world geography.

But even as I'm wishing
I'm working faithfully
To be the best kid anywhere
By simply being me!

Dear Wally,

Is God going to come down to earth and rapture us up to heaven in the year 2000? And is it true that the devil will take some people down to hell in the fiery brimstone and you will never die? And up in heaven there will be streets of gold and some mansions? And the people there will never cry even though some of their family are in hell? I would like to know.

Your friend,

Betsy

"Is God going to come down to earth and rapture us up to heaven in the year 2000?"

Dear Betsy,

You have been doing some heavy thinking—and that's good!

Yes, Jesus is coming back to earth. When will this happen? In the year 2000? Tomorrow? The Bible tells us, "No one knows about that day or hour, not even the angels in heaven" (Matthew 24:36, NIV). And when He does, He will take all the believers back to heaven with Him. There will be mansions and streets of gold. Best of all, God will light up the whole place just by being there!

I can't explain why we won't cry in heaven—but we won't. There will be no tears or sadness, only joy and laughter and incredible brightness. God will make sure of that!

Just as heaven is a real place, so is hell. It is a place of pain and misery and separation from God. And there evil people will suffer forever.

The important thing is not *when* all this is going to happen, but that it *is* going to happen! So instead of sitting on a park bench and waiting for the skies to split open, God wants us to stay busy living full, good lives "because you do not know on what day your Lord will come" (Matthew 24:42, NIV).

WALLY

Dear Wally,

I have a problem about lying and cheating. And I want to stop! If you could pray for me I would really appreciate it please. Thanks.

Whitney

Dear Whitney,

Do you know the hardest thing about changing your behavior? Admitting you need to change. And you've already done that!

Have you ever tried to break a bad habit? Maybe biting your nails or watching too much TV? It's not easy! Habits become habits because you do them over and over and over—until you just do them without thinking. Maybe lying and cheating are becoming like that for you. And you need to stop now. The longer you wait, the harder it will be.

Nothing good ever comes from dishonesty, Whitney. And it makes you feel miserable, doesn't it? That churning inside you is your conscience—sort of a built-in radar system to steer you away from sin. And the Bible makes it clear that lying and cheating are sin.

It sounds like you know God wants to help you. Ask Him to make you strong enough to do what's right. "'If we confess our sins, he is faithful and just and will forgive us our sins and purify us from all unrighteousness" (1 John 1:9, NIV). Then, with His help, you must do whatever is necessary so it won't happen again. Do you need to make some new friends? Ask to sit somewhere else at school? Talk to an adult you trust? Whatever you need to do, do it!

We're praying for you—and believing in you too.

WALLY

WHAT'S A FRIEND TO DO?

What would you do if a friend asked you to help him cheat on a test? Suppose all you had to do was write big and not cover up your answers. What if no one would ever know? After all, all you're really doing is helping out a buddy....

Hold it! Your friend's biggest problem is not his schoolwork. It's the fact that he's planning to do something dishonest. And he wants you to be part of the scheme. Not only will you be cheating, but you'll be helping him lie to the teacher—telling her, through his test score, that he knows and understands things he doesn't. Then your friend will get even further behind.

Listen to your conscience, that voice inside you waving a red flag and telling you to stop. It's God's way of helping you stay away from sin. And don't be fooled into thinking no one will know. Even if you fool your teacher, *you* will know what you've done. God will know too.

So say a prayer for God's help, take a deep breath, and tell your friend that you don't cheat. Then offer to help him study.

It's what a real friend does.

Dear Wally,

I have a problem with piano. I really do like piano a lot but sometimes I wish I could just quit. I know the right thing is probably just to work at it. But a lot of the time I just don't want to practice, and then my mom has to say to me, "Meg, go practice your piano." I'm trying to start reminding myself to do it, but it's really hard. What do you think I should do—keep playing the piano or quit?

Your new friend,

Meg

P.S. It was nice meeting you! Bye!

Dear Meg,

How lucky you are to be able to play the piano! We turtles have to stick to whistling. (The only thing I know how to play is the radio!)

You sound like the kind of person who wants to succeed. And what determines success—in any area—is not so much talent as it is discipline.

Once you've committed yourself to a project, give it your all. If you've decided you want to be able to play the piano (a skill you can enjoy for the rest of your life!), then practice. If playing professional tennis is your dream, put in your court time. Want to win your school's spelling bee? Study the word lists. A chart can help you organize your time and keep track of your commitments. You might even reward yourself with gold stars or sticks of gum.

Sticking with what you start is tough, but it's almost always worth it. "Finishing is better than starting! Patience is better than pride!" (Ecclesiastes 7:8, TLB).

WALLY

Dear Wally,

My parents have been divorced for two years now, and it has been hard on me, especially since my mom is giving me less freedom. My life is really torn apart. I'm thinking of moving in with my dad, since I can visit my mom whenever I want instead of going every Wednesday, every other Thursday, and weekends. I know I am lucky I get to see my mom and dad so much, but my grades are going down. My situation is tougher now than it was two years ago. I think that since my mom and dad are fighting more (even through letters and on the phone) it's having an effect on me. What should I do?

Truly yours,

April

P.S. Please write back.

Dear April,

Divorce is never easy. It means new rules and constant squabbles and a hurt in your heart that won't go away. You're smart to realize how lucky you are to get to see both parents as much as you do.

About your parents fighting—the arguments are between *them*. They are not your fault and you cannot stop them. Don't take sides. If possible, leave the scene when the fighting begins. Go to your room, take a walk, visit a friend. Don't become their audience.

About moving in with your dad—don't be fooled into thinking that things will be perfect there, or even better. You may have more freedom, but you may be lonelier too.

About your grades—get them up! Falling behind in your schoolwork will only give you another giant set of problems to deal with. Let your parents work out their problems. Your job is to get good grades and grow up loving them both.

And remember that you've always got someone to talk to, someone who never changes no matter how much everything else does. "The God of all comfort, who comforts us in all our troubles, so that we can comfort those in any trouble with the comfort we ourselves have received from God" (2 Corinthians 1:3-4, NIV). Who knows, maybe you'll be able to pass some of that comfort on to your folks.

WALLY

TOUGH FACTS FOR KIDS ABOUT DIVORCE

1. It's not your fault. You didn't cause the divorce and you can't fix it.
2. Your parents probably won't get married to each other again.
3. You can be happy living with one parent. Adjust to the changes.
4. You are loved! Your parents may have stopped loving each other, but they haven't stopped loving you. And they never will.
5. Your family has changed, but you're still a family.
6. Divorce doesn't just happen to bad kids.
7. It's normal to feel lonely, angry, sad, embarrassed and guilty—all at the same time. Things will get better!
8. Talking about your feelings can help you deal with them.
9. You can love both parents. You don't have to take sides.
10. You are loved! (It's worth repeating!)

Dear Wally,

I have a problem. Actually it's everybody's problem. It's about how animals are treated. Some are raised in pet mills and sold. Others are used in labs for experiments. Surely the Lord did not make animals to be sold for a profit and treated as a piece of merchandise. Help me save animals!

Sincerely,

Casey

For over a hundred years, the American Society for the Prevention of Cruelty to Animals (sometimes called the ASPCA) has been helping lost or unwanted animals. Last year, in New York City alone, they cared for over 100,000 animals!

Dear Casey,

It's great that you care about animals. Specs and I think "BE KIND TO ANIMALS WEEK" should last all year long! And you're right—the way animals are treated is everyone's concern. God made it that way in the Garden of Eden when He created man and told him to "Rule over . . . every living creature" (Genesis 1:28, NIV).

But part of that "ruling over" means that man has always used animals—for plowing fields so he could grow crops, for producing eggs and milk, even for meat. Now animals are used for scientific research. In the United States alone, 20 million animals—most of them rats—are in laboratory cages. And sometimes that means they aren't treated kindly.

There are laws to protect these animals, to make sure they are not abused in the process of the experiments. And it is important work. Every medicine—from allergy capsules to heart pills—was first tested on animals. But it's still hard not to feel sorry for them.

You may want to write to your congressman or other legislators. (Your librarian can help you find their names and addresses.) Tell them you think the laws need to protect animals and punish the people who mistreat them. You might even write a letter to the editor of your school or local newspaper.

And speaking for turtles—and all God's other creatures—thanks for the help!

WALLY

How to Take Care of a Pet

Feeding - Make sure your pet gets the right kind of food. (Just because you like pepperoni pizza doesn't mean it's a good thing to feed to your dog!) Buy foods prepared especially for the animal. Rabbit pellets, dry dog food, canned cat food—even frozen baby mice for snakes—are available at your local supermarket or pet store. And all animals need plenty of fresh water.

Grooming - Most pets need to be brushed and bathed often. Watch for any signs of ticks or fleas. If your pet lives in a confined area, like a cage or bowl or stall, remember to clean it regularly.

Loving - Give your pet the attention it needs—and deserves. Exercise and play with it every day. Make sure your cat or dog has a collar with identification tags in case he gets lost. Treat your pet the way you'd like to be treated!

Dear Wally,

I've got this problem. I have freckles on my face, legs, and arms. Everyone at school calls me "Freckle Face"! What should I do?

Amy

Dear Amy,

I love freckles. Of course, that's probably because I don't have to wear them on my nose every day. I'm sorry the kids tease you. And they probably won't stop—as long as they know it bothers you. Freckle Face isn't such a terrible nickname, as nicknames go. It's not exaggerated or nasty. In fact, it's based on a biological fact—you *do* have freckles. (You think it's easy for me to put up with all those jokes about how slow turtles are?)

Nobody is totally happy with the way she looks. And if other kids pick up on that, they begin teasing you about whatever it is you don't like about yourself. In your case, that's freckles. God knows about your freckles, Amy. In fact, He created them! You were "wonderfully made" to God's specifications (Psalm 139:14, NIV).

This is tough advice to follow, but it's the only solution to your problem: Ignore the "freckle-face" comments. When someone says, "You have freckles!" laugh back and say, "You noticed!" Soon you'll find people aren't laughing at you, they're laughing *with* you.

WALLY

Dear Wally,

I have a big problem. Everyone in my class has had a boyfriend or a girlfriend. I've never had a boyfriend ever, NOT EVEN IN KINDERGARTEN!! I'm very sad. Can you help me?

Your pal,

Elizabeth

P.S. I'm in fifth grade.

Did you know there is more than one kind of love? In fact, there's even more than two kinds of love...

♦One kind is the love we have for each other, the love that makes us want to help each other and be kind to one another.

♦Another is the love that men and women share, a special physical attraction that brings them together in marriage.

♦And the most important love of all is God's love. It's always there for us—even when we mess up!

Dear Elizabeth,

What would you think if your mother told you that this year you were all going to celebrate Christmas on the Fourth of July? Or if your best friend had her birthday party three months early? That would be pretty silly, wouldn't it? But no sillier than doing other things before it's time—things like having boyfriends and girlfriends.

"There is a right time for everything" (Ecclesiastes 3:1, TLB)—and the time to have a boyfriend or a girl-friend is not in elementary school! Your friends who are doing this are just pretending, imitating their older broth-ers and sisters or the teens they see on TV. Now is the time for group activities and lots of friends of both sexes. Parties and ball games, group projects and trips to the mall, hiking and volleyball. There's lots of fun things to do that take more than two!

So stop feeling sad. You're not behind. You're right on schedule. And someday, when you're a young adult, God will bring special people into your life for you to care about. And you'll be glad you waited.

WALLY

Dear Wally,
    I have a friend named Nancy. She always rummages through other people's things. I'm afraid that if I stick with her I'm going to get blamed for her actions.

Megan

Dear Megan,

Did you know that when a ship sinks it sucks in everything around it? Whatever happens to be close to the ship goes down with it. And it sounds like your friend may be a "sinking ship."

Whether it's fair or not, people judge us by our friends. If our friends are fun and honest and helpful, people think we are too. But if our friends are cruel or self-centered or dishonest, that's what other people believe us to be. The old saying "birds of a feather flock together" is usually true. Friends are friends because they're a lot alike. And you're right—if you stick with Nancy, you're going to get blamed too.

Maybe you can get Nancy to stop her bad habit. The next time she begins to rummage through someone's things, look her in the eye and say, "Nancy, why are you doing this?" As her friend, you have the right to know. Warn her that she is headed for big trouble—loss of friends, trips to the principal's office, bad feelings about herself. Then, if Nancy still insists on doing this, walk away from her. Don't be anywhere nearby when she is doing what she's not supposed to!

The Bible tells us that "Bad company corrupts good character" (1 Corinthians 15:33, NIV). Don't let that happen to you!

Get your friend to change her behavior—or change friends.

WALLY

65

Dear Wally,

Hi, my name is Brandon. I'm 12 years old and going into the seventh grade. I have this problem. I wear very thick glasses, so it makes my eyes look bigger than my face. People at school sometimes kid me about it. I know people say it matters only what you look like on the inside, not on the outside. And I think that's true. But other people don't take the time to recognize that. Please give me some advice on what to do.

Your friend,

Brandon

SOME SHADY CHARACTERS

Sunglasses. Long before skateboarders or movie stars wore them, they had a different use.

It was in China in the early fifteenth century that glass was first smoked and used for eyewear, but it had nothing to do with sunshine. These special glasses were used by Chinese judges to conceal their eyes during trials. It was thought that a judge's feelings about the evidence should be kept secret. And since they were afraid the eyes would betray the emotions, each judge wore the smoked glasses until the trial was over.

Dear Brandon,

You're a pretty smart kid! Lots of adults haven't figured out what you already know—it's what you are on the inside that matters most. And you're also right about other people not taking the time to realize this.

You're probably also smart enough to know that you can't control what other people do. Even if there were laws against making fun of others, some people would still do it. They try to make themselves feel big by cutting down everybody else. Or they try to be the center of attention with their witty—and sometimes cruel—comments. They need to learn to "Do to others as you would have them do to you" (Luke 6:31, NIV).

What you can control, though, is how you respond to what people say. If you get upset, it's like throwing sticks on a campfire. So be calm on the outside (even if you're steaming on the inside). Don't give the teasers the attention or satisfaction they want. Soon they'll tire of the "bug-eyed" comments. And if they're smart, they'll find out what a neat kid you are—inside and out!

WALLY

Dear Wally,
    I've got a problem. My mom and dad got divorced last year. Right now I'm living with my dad and my sister lives with my mom. In May on Memorial Day my mom's getting married. They want to adopt me! What should I do?

                                    Your friend,

                                    Sharon

Dear Sharon,

Adoption is a very special thing! It means that you have been chosen, that someone wants you very much.

The "family" you're being asked to join is mostly your family already. Your mom, your sister, and now a new stepfather. What you're feeling may be sadness about moving, or even a fear that you may hurt your dad's feelings. Sharon, adoption is a legal act. Love is a free gift. And you'll still be free to give just as much love as you want to your real dad.

Did you know that all of us Christians have already been adopted? It's true! "His [God's] unchanging plan has always been to adopt us into his own family by sending Jesus Christ to die for us. And he did this because he wanted to!" (Ephesians 1:5, TLB). That makes us brothers and sisters with Jesus. And that's why "we should behave like God's very own children, adopted into . . . his family" (Romans 8:15, TLB).

Although you feel confused right now, you're really lucky. Lots of people love you and want you. So no matter what your last name is or who has legal guardianship of you, you will still have lots of family. And your "Big Brother," Jesus, will be right there anytime you need to talk.

WALLY

Dear Wally,

I have a problem. My grandfather is dying slowly. He is in and out of the hospital, and I'm scared! Sometimes I want to cry when I see him, but I hold it in. He may die any day. What should I do?

Cathy

"I have a problem. My grandfather is dying slowly."

Dear Cathy,

Watching someone you love die is the hardest thing you will ever have to do. It makes you feel both scared and helpless.

Let's talk first about the scared part. What exactly are you scared of? If it's the pain your grandfather is suffering, know that his doctors are taking care of that. They know just what to do to make him as comfortable as possible. What you're probably most scared of is losing your grandfather to death—that strange thing we know little about. But we do know this: "Those who walk uprightly enter into peace; they find rest as they lie in death" (Isaiah 57:2, NIV). Life is only a small part of reality. The bigger—and for those who love the Lord, the better—part lies ahead, after death.

Now, about what you can do. Read to your grandfather. Tell him what you're doing in school. Visit him as much as possible. Share happy memories with him—a birthday party or sled ride or face-licking puppy. Even after a person has lost the ability to talk, he can usually hear. And your voice would be a real comfort to him. Hold his hand, hug him, let him know you're close by.

It's only natural to be scared and not want to be around your grandfather. When things seem especially difficult, remember this—death is not the end. It is the beginning. Christ tells us, "I am the resurrection and the life. He who believes in me will live, even though he dies" (John 11:25, NIV).

I'm so sorry about your grandfather, Cathy.

WALLY

Dear Wally,

I've got a problem with tests at school. I study the night before a test (or earlier), and I get an "F." I get an "F" on almost every test. My teacher and I are trying to figure out a way that I can remember the stuff for my tests. Do you have any ideas on what I could do to remember the stuff?

Dale

Dear Dale,

Feeling nervous about a test is normal. Even Specs gets the jitters—and he's the smartest creature I know! It may sound silly, but studying for a test really begins long before the test. Pay attention in class. The teacher will give you clues about what's going to be on the test. Know the kinds of questions to expect. Will there be multiple choice? T & F? Will you need to know names and dates? Take notes; ask questions.

Specs has some good advice too. Don't try to cram everything into one night. Give yourself several review sessions. Study illustrations, maps, graphs. They highlight important people, events, details, facts. Review headings and subheadings. Read the questions at the end of the chapter. Can you answer them? Go over vocabulary words or any italicized words.

And don't forget to pray. God cares about everything in your life—including tests! He wants you to "be strong and courageous and get to work. Don't be frightened by the size of the task, for the Lord God is with you..." (1 Chronicles 28:20, TLB). Do your best, and He'll help with the rest!

WALLY

TEN TIPS FOR TAKING TESTS (AND DOING YOUR BEST!)

1. Get plenty of sleep the night before. Eat breakfast—and not just donuts and presweetened cereal! How about eggs or waffles, peanut butter on toast or even a cheese sandwich?
2. Make sure you have all the supplies you need—pencils, paper, books, notes, maps. Whatever!
3. Be sure you understand the directions on the test. Don't be afraid to ask your teacher to explain anything you don't understand.
4. Do the easy questions first. Skip any you're unsure of. (Then come back to them later.)
5. Be neat.
6. Write down something for every question.
7. If your mind begins to wander, stop and count to ten. Stay calm.
8. Use all of your test time. Make sure you leave enough time for each question. Don't hurry! Being the first one done isn't what counts. Doing the best you can is.
9. Look over your finished paper before handing it in.
10. Expect to do well.

Dear Wally,

I have a problem with Tom. Every time my soccer team wins, he will say, "You cheated. I hate you." Then he will try to punch me, and I will run away, and he will say I'm a chicken. What should I do?

Shawn

Have you ever seen a big bull stomping back and forth, bellowing and snorting? That's where the expression "bully" comes from.

Dear Shawn,

Bullies have been around for a long time. Remember that gruesome Goliath who had the whole army of Israel shaking in their sandals until David came along?

How does Tom treat you the rest of the time? Is he friendly? Does he only bully you when your team's won and his has lost? Sounds like Tom's biggest problem is being a poor sport. And he takes all his anger about losing and directs it at someone else. Unfortunately, that someone's you.

Try staying away from Tom after a winning game. Don't rub it in that your team beat his. When *his* team wins, show him how a good sport should act. Congratulate him. Shake his hand. If Tom still tries to fight you, tell him, "We have nothing to fight about. The game is over and there will be another one tomorrow. Sometimes you win and sometimes you lose. That's just the way it is." Then turn and *walk* away. Avoiding a fight doesn't make you "chicken." It makes you smart! The Bible tells us that "the fruit of the Spirit is. . . peace" (Galatians 5:22, NIV). Anybody can punch and kick, but it takes real courage to refuse to fight.

Usually bullies give up if they don't get what they want. But if things don't get better between you and Tom, talk it over with your teacher or your dad.

WALLY

SOMETIMES IT HELPS TO HAVE A TOUGH SHELL.

Dear Wally,

My eyes are not seeing as good as they used to. No one believes me. Everything is blurry. I have to blink a lot too. Can you help me?

P.S. I can't stand it!

Kari

Dear Kari,

Your eyes are *very* important. In fact, the Bible calls them "the lamp of the body" (Matthew 6:22, NIV). If you are having a problem seeing, you need to talk to someone right away. The school nurse is a good place to begin. She has charts that will help her determine if your eyes need special attention. She may suggest a trip to the *optometrist* (eye doctor). It could be that you have a temporary problem—maybe an infection or even a piece of dirt or sand stuck in your eye. The nurse, or another adult you trust, may be able to help by giving you eye-drops or other medicine.

Talk to your teacher about this problem. Tell your parents. Don't whine or cry, but make sure they realize that you are scared and need their help. Most eye problems can be corrected—so keep telling people until someone helps you take care of this problem.

WALLY

B**O**rn to Blink

      Did you know that you blink your eyes every 2 to 10 seconds? That's as many as 30 blinks a minute! And it's a good thing you do, because blinking helps keep your eyes healthy. Here's how it works: Your eyelids, by opening and closing, keep your eyes clean. So do tears. Even when you're not crying, they're in your eyes. Blinking helps spread them over your eyes and wash off dirt. These spread-out tears also keep your eyes from drying out. And if you've ever played dodge ball or ducked out of the way of a paper wad, you know that one of the most important jobs of blinking is to keep your eyes safe when something comes too close to them.

Dear Wally,

My best friend has only one friend at school—me. The kids at school don't like her because her hair is curly and sometimes very tangly. They say she dresses like a nerd. And some of the boys at school make fun of me because I'm her friend. I don't like the way they treat her. What should I do?

Ashleigh

Dear Ashleigh,

Yeah for you! You're the kind of friend every kid wants to have. Did you know the Bible has a lot to say about friendship? Ecclesiastes 4:10 (NIV) talks about how important it is. "If [some]one falls down, his friend can help him up. But pity the man who falls and has no one to help him up!"

Keep on being friends with your friend. Pick her for teams, sit with her at lunch, send her valentines and birthday invitations. Maybe the other kids will begin to see the good things about her, the things that make her your best friend. But if they don't, if the teasing keeps up, there's something you should know. You and your friend aren't losers or nerds. Those labels are for people who can't see past the outside, for loudmouths who make fun of everything they don't understand.

How lucky your friend is to have someone like you!

WALLY

Dear Wally

I want to help fight the drug war, but I don't know how. I know God said to do your best always, but that's not helping me. Please help me!

Josh

Dear Josh,

Good for you! The war against drugs needs all the soldiers it can get! Here's how you can help:

- Don't take drugs yourself. And don't hang around with people who do. If a friend tries to get you to try some, say *no*. Suggest the two of you do something else instead. If he insists, say something like, "I don't do drugs. I'm leaving now, but if you want to see me later I'll be at home" (or wherever). If he keeps pushing drugs on you, find a new friend.
- If you know someone who is selling drugs, tell an adult you trust—your principal or pastor or social worker.
- Don't wear T-shirts that glamorize drugs. Don't buy (or listen to) tapes that encourage drug use. Drugs are a serious thing! Don't be a part of anything that makes them look cool or harmless.
- Join an anti-drug group. Or you and your friends start your own "Kids Against Drugs" club. You could design special membership T-shirts or buttons. Each member could sign a pledge like the one on the next page.

With soldiers like you, I know we can win the drug war.

WALLY

PLEDGE CARD

Because I know that my "body is a temple of the Holy Spirit" (1 Corinthians 6:19, NIV), I will...

1. Say "NO!" to harmful drugs.
2. Help my friends to say no too.
3. Stand up for what I know is right.

_____

Dear Wally,

I am hoping you will be able to help me. My name is Gretchen. I am 11 years old. My problem is a big one. It is a little over four feet tall, has blond hair, blue eyes, and is 9 years old. That is my little sister, Kim.

She is always annoying me. We have to share a room. For the past few months my side of the room is her garbage can. If she doesn't feel like putting things away, she throws them on my bed.

Also, whenever something goes wrong she puts on a "Little Miss Innocent" face. Then I get yelled at. I need help!!!

Gretchen

P.S. My stuff is continuously disappearing, for instance my diary.

KEEP OUT!
NO SISTERS
ALLOWED

Dear Gretchen,

There are lots of things I like about being a turtle. And after reading your letter, not having to share my "shell" is one of them!

The Bible counsels us to "Live in harmony with one another" (Romans 12:16, NIV). But it sounds like you and Kim are making some pretty *inharmonious* sounds right now! What you need is a plan of action . . .

1. Don't trash Kim's things to get even. If her sweater is lying on the floor, pick it up instead of stepping on it.

2. Don't nag. It almost never works. Remember the "show and tell" sessions from kindergarten? Almost everybody liked the "show" part best. So *show* Kim how you'd like to be treated by treating her that way. And praise even the smallest effort at cleaning up or getting along on her part.

3. Offer to help her clean up her side of the room. Maybe she's just overwhelmed by the mess. Together tackle the piles and clutter. Chances are she'll feel a certain pride once everything is neat—a pride that may help her keep it that way.

4. Ask your parents for your own special place to keep your most private things. A metal box with a lock would work well.

5. Talk to your parents. Explain to them that your privacy is important. As a family, brainstorm ways to protect both yours and Kim's rights.

Who knows, with some hard work and understanding, you and Kim may be able to make some harmony after all!

WALLY

Dear Wally,
    Me, my dad, and my mom always get mad at each other. I always think about running away, but when, where, how long? I could just sleep behind the garage and scare them. I'm in my room now for yelling at my mom.

Daniel

Every day more than 3,000 kids run away from home—but not to "happily ever after" endings . . . .

Dear Daniel,

I once thought about running away from home. But when you're a turtle and carry your "home" around on your back, it's kind of hard to run away! And problems are like my shell—you'll have them no matter where you go.

Of course, some people do leave home. Every day more than *3,000* kids run away, but not to "happily ever after" endings. Lots of them end up on the streets, where it's easy to get involved in drugs, stealing, and other illegal activities.

Sounds like you and your folks need to have a long talk. Why do you get mad at each other? What can each of you do to make the situation better? Try to "be kind and compassionate to one another" (Ephesians 4:32, NIV). Chances are, no *one* person is to blame. And working *together* can make things lots better at home.

It may help you to talk about this with a teacher or counselor at school. But don't run away! (And sleeping behind the garage is *not* a good idea.) You'll find even bigger problems waiting for you if you do.

WALLY

Dear Wally,

My dad drinks alcohol. At nights he is very drunk. And he acts like he is strangling me and my mom. Sometimes he really scares me, a lot. What should I do?

Nicole

Drinking can cause serious problems, both physical and emotional, especially in young people. And studies show that lots of kids—some as young as 11 years old—are experimenting with alcohol. But it's a dumb thing to do! Here's why:

● Alcohol can interfere with normal growth patterns. Using alcohol can create a chemical imbalance that slows down the development of your whole body, especially the muscles. Your body needs good nutrition so it can develop strong bones and healthy tissue!

● Young people can become addicted to alcohol faster than older people. (When a person is addicted to something, he wants it more than anything else. That need takes over his life and becomes more important than work or friends or church.) An adult may take 5-15 years to develop alcoholism, but a teenager can become addicted in only 6-18 *months!*

● *You don't have to drink to have fun!* That's a good rule to remember—whether you're 9 or 90!

Dear Nicole,

Do you know what a *mobile* is? Sometimes classrooms have them hanging from the ceiling. They're art forms made from rods and string with different shapes hanging from them—colored leaves or snowflakes or zoo animals. The whole thing moves together whenever it is stirred by the wind or bumped by a passing hand. The pieces are connected—one piece can't be jarred without all the pieces feeling the vibrations. Families are like that too. Your father's drinking problem has become a *family* problem. You and your mother, connected to him by strings of love and responsibility, are being bounced around with his drunkenness and temper.

Whenever you see that your father is beginning to drink too much, get out of his way. Ask your mom for permission to go to a friend or relative's house. If that isn't possible, go to your room.

It's important that you and your mom pray for your dad. Alcohol has become more important to him than anything else. The Bible warns us not to be deceived by the "sparkle and smooth taste" of alcohol. "For in the end it bites like a poisonous serpent" (Proverbs 23:31-32, TLB).

But you need to put action behind your prayers. Tell your mother how frightened you are, Nicole. Ask her about taking you to a counselor. Maybe you could talk to your teacher or principal. Ministers often have good advice. This problem is too big for you to handle alone. You and your mother need professional help. Loving your father won't make his problems—or yours—go away.

WALLY

Dear Wally,
     I have this big problem. See, I am about ten pounds overweight, and I've been fasting for one and a half days and doing a lot of running and exercise stuff. Everyone says I am very pretty, but if that's so how come I can't get a boyfriend? Please help!

                                        Holly

Dear Holly,

I'm glad you wrote to me! You seem to be confused about a couple of things . . . .

The first is how to lose weight. Fasting is not a good way to diet! When you suddenly stop eating, your body shifts into low gear and burns only enough calories to survive. Fasting can be *very* dangerous unless done under a doctor's care. And most people who fast to lose weight get discouraged and then binge on the wrong foods. Exercise, of course, is good, but if you are denying your body the proper nutrition and forcing it to exercise, you are probably burning muscle tissue, not fat. And that's not good! The best way to lose weight is by eating foods low in fat and combining that with regular aerobic exercise.

The second thing that you're confused about is the relationship between being pretty and having boyfriends. One has little to do with the other! People like people who are bright and friendly, witty and warm, clever and caring. Boys are no different. They look for these qualities in girls, too. Sure, pretty girls get lots of attention. But it takes more than looks to create a real relationship with someone.

Holly, the best thing you can to is to like yourself more. Don't let other people decide your worth. And don't let a boy's attention, or lack of it, determine whether or not you're attractive. Work on what you want to change about yourself, but be glad for the things about you that are good.

You are "wonderfully made" (Psalm 139:14, NIV)—a unique, much-loved child of God. Don't forget that! And once you start liking yourself better, you'll be surprised how many other people (some of them boys!) will like you too.

Does it seem like everybody runs faster than you do, gets better grades in math, and has more friends? Do you feel like an ugly duckling in a pond of swans? Then it's time you learned...

HOW TO LIKE YOURSELF MORE

1. Make a list of your best qualities. Write them down! Are you honest? Do you have a sense of humor? Can you toss a ball or play a sonata?

2. Now make a list of your most obvious faults. Call it: "Needs Improvement." Are you quick to blame other people? Do you have trouble getting up on school-day mornings? Do you interrupt? Burp at the table?

   Now decide which one is the most important, which one you want most to change. Then devise a plan to work on it. Set realistic goals. Give yourself time. If you tend to be rude to your older sister, every day for a week compliment her. If you bite your nails, let your goal be to stop biting them for three days. After you've made progress on a particular point, move on to another. Remember, work on only one "fault" at a time.

3. Develop your strong points even more. If you are a good group worker, volunteer to help with class projects. If you like to sew, try making a surprise apron or scarf for your mother.

4. Act in ways that make you feel good about yourself. Control your temper. Share your dessert. Do an extra chore. Finish your homework.

5. Don't compare yourself to others. Be the best *you* can be!

What I like about me:

_____

_____

_____

_____

_____

_____

Needs improvement:

_____

_____

_____

_____

_____

_____

Dear Wally,

   I am having a lot of trouble getting along with my mom. I don't know why she yells at me for wanting to play football. She acts like I'm going to get killed when I play. I always play at school. By the way, I am 9 years old. I am the best player at school, and I also beat fifth graders at football.

Nathan

Dear Nathan,

I've noticed that human mothers can be a pain—always telling you to wear a jacket or take a bath or do your homework! And every mother has a special something she worries about. Have you talked to your mom about why she hates football so much? Maybe she's worried about broken bones and bloody noses. And if she is, that makes her . . . human! All moms worry about stuff like that. Know why? Because they love their kids and don't want to see them get hurt.

Let me ask you something, Nathan. *Why* do you want to play football? Is it because you really like that sport? Is it a "power play" to see if you can get your mom to let you? Or do you want to feel *big*? You know, you don't have to play football to be important or popular. Once you know what makes football so important to you, why not sit down with your mom and talk it over with her?

Fighting about the issue will get you nowhere—except maybe grounded in your room. Try a different approach. When the two of you go shopping, take her to a sports store and let her see how padded all that football gear really is! Maybe one of the other kids who plays could get his mom to talk to yours about the sport—about how it helps you be more disciplined and learn about teamwork. Or the coach of the team might tell her how much time they spend on proper training and equipment.

The Bible says to "honor your father and your mother" (Exodus 20:12, NIV). What does that mean? Well, for one thing it means the best way to win your mother over is to respect her wishes and do as she says. That doesn't mean football will stop being important to you. But if you show your mother you're responsible and reasonable—she'll be reasonable too!

WALLY

Dear Wally,

I have a friend who is not nice to people who aren't popular in my school. She goes around telling people that they are snobs and that they should be in a retarded school. One time when she said that, I asked her if she would feel bad if someone said that to her. But she still does it, and in front of me! And she thinks it's funny! What should I do?

Denise

Dear Denise,

What powerful things words are! They can make new friends, break down walls of shyness, pass along a funny joke or a special wish. They can also hurt people. And the hurts are deeper than skinned knees or scraped elbows.

Why does your friend go around deliberately hurting other people's feelings? Does it make her feel important? Better than them? Even if you don't join in, you're part of the situation just by the fact that you're with your friend when she acts like this. The Bible warns us to stay away from "all appearance of evil" (1 Thessalonians 5:22, KJV).

When people act in a way you don't approve of, it's right to let them know, especially if that person is a friend. You've done that—good for you! But now it's time to do even more.

You can't keep excusing your friend's actions, hoping she'll change. Whenever she starts calling someone a "snob," turn and walk away from her. Tell her you don't want to be a part of name-calling. You may find yourself spending less time with her, especially at first. But if your friendship is important to her, she'll stop making fun of people. And who knows, you may find there are other friends you can enjoy even more, friends who go around speaking *happy* instead of hurtful words!

WALLY

Dear Wally,

I've read your answers, and I think you give some good advice. I am 14 years old and really confused. Could you please help me out with a problem I have?

Last year—on July 27—me and my brother stole a car. Since then I've been put in shelters, group homes, detention centers, and the State Training School for Boys. I've been to hell and back, but the people where I live won't forgive me for stealing the car. They keep giving me the "cold shoulder." What should I do to get them to like me again?

Kip

"Last year me and my brother stole a car."

Dear Kip,

Forgiveness is so important—and so *hard*! But before we talk about other people, let's talk about you. What you did—stealing the car—was bad, but that doesn't make *you* bad. Don't be suckered into thinking: "They all think I'm a jerk so I might as well act like one." Respect yourself! Be friendly, not defensive. Treat the people who are snubbing you the way you *want* them to treat you.

Respect and trust are things all of us have to *earn*. And once you violate that trust by doing unacceptable things, it's hard to regain it. Be the best you can be *all the time*. Speak the best you can speak *all the time* (no profanity!). Do the best you can *all the time*. Sound tough? Sure—but with God's help you can do it! "And let us not get tired of doing what is right, for after a while we will reap a harvest of blessing if we don't get discouraged and give up" (Galatians 6:9, TLB).

There are only three people whose forgiveness it is essential you seek. The first, of course, is God's. He's ready when you are. The second is the person from whom you stole the car. Write and say you're sorry. The third person who must forgive you is—*you*. Don't keep beating yourself over the head for past mistakes. Get on with life. And be willing to forgive the people who are finding it hard to forgive you.

I can tell you're an intelligent guy. Don't let what others think determine how you live your life. You are God's special child. Why not let Him help you become all He wants you to be?

WALLY

Dear Wally,

I have had lots of problems lately. First, my mom and dad divorced, and that is one of the most terrible things. Second, we are becoming poor because my dad won't give us any money. And we are also having to move. I am in need of some help. Please help me!

Colby

Dear Colby,

Did you ever toss a pebble into a pond and watch what happens? From that one *plunk* in the water, ripples go out in all directions. Divorce can be like that—from that one big problem come lots of other changes.

About money—it's good to have some. And there are ways you can earn your own spending cash. Do yard work for the neighbors, take a paper route, help a farmer with his milking or haying, shovel snow, pet sit for friends on vacation, wash windows, have a yard sale.

But the most important things in life have little to do with money. Your health, knowing people love you, the sun on your face as you race your bike down a hill, counting stars on a night so clear you feel you could touch the skies. "Keep your lives free from the love of money and be content with what you have, because God has said, 'Never will I leave you; never will I forsake you'" (Hebrews 13:5, NIV). Think about the things you *do* have, not just the things you don't. Help your mom out by not asking for things she can't afford—and you don't really need.

About the move—sometimes moves can be good. Maybe your new place will be less expensive, and you and your mom will have some dollars left over for fun things. Perhaps you'll meet new friends—friends who may be waiting and hoping someone just like *you* will move into their apartment building or onto their block.

Problems are no fun, Colby. But sometimes they do open up new possibilities. A different neighborhood, a part-time job, new friends. Sounds like an adventure is waiting for you!

WALLY

FUN THINGS TO DO THAT ARE (ALMOST) FREE

● fly a kite

■ visit a museum

▲ take a hike and see how many kinds of birds you can see

● ride your bike

■ kick or bounce or toss a ball

▲ join a group at school or church

● draw

▲ play tag with your friends

■ jump rope

● make popcorn and invite friends over to do a puzzle

▲ swim

■ build a sand castle

● read

▲ make an egg-carton garden (Directions: Using an empty egg carton, fill with good black dirt and plant some seeds; water daily.)

■ climb a tree

▲ go on a picnic

● get a "things-to-make" book from the library

■ play jacks

▲ volunteer at your local YMCA or senior citizen's center

● go to the zoo

■ play board games

Dear Wally,

I've got this problem. There's this new boy. I feel sorry for him. I want to ask him to play and to tell him about Jesus. But I get too nervous. What should I do?

Ross

Dear Ross,

Believe it or not, I used to be shy. I spent more time with my head inside my shell than outside it! And it kept me from having fun—and helping people.

It's good that you're thinking about this new boy. (He probably feels a little nervous too.) Try to put aside your own fears and jitters and concentrate on how he must feel . . . leaving behind his old friends, having to go to a different school, living in a new neighborhood. Then gather your courage and ask him to play. He's probably hoping you will! Maybe after a game of catch the two of you can share a candy bar or a bunch of grapes. Little by little, day by day, get to know him—and let him get to know you. In fact, that's the best way you can "tell" him about Jesus: let him see Jesus in the way you act, "in your love, your faith, and your clean thoughts" (1 Timothy 4:12, TLB).

And since it's only natural for friends to go places together, soon you can ask him to go to church with you. There he can learn even more about your Friend!

WALLY

1. Make eye contact with people when they talk to you. Look straight into their eyes—and you'll see yourself looking back. That's not so scary, is it? Eye contact not only lets the other person know you're interested in what he's saying, it actually helps you listen better.

2. Compliment someone. Tell a classmate you liked his book report. Comment on what a cute sweater your friend is wearing. Thank the bus driver for your ride to school.

3. Do a favor for someone. Pick up a dropped book, open a jammed locker, loan a sharpened pencil, share a special dessert. And if *you* need a favor—ask for it!

4. Tell a joke. Practice until you can tell it really well. Then next time you're in a group—give it a try! (Do you know why Cinderella was kicked off the baseball team? She ran away from the ball!)

5. Trust other people. Expect to be liked. Don't spend your life waiting for the worst to happen. Sometimes you will strike out—but lots of times you won't.

Dear Wally,
    This may seem like a silly question, but I was wondering if it is possible to go back in time. I want to know because I could try to make my life better.

Randy

Scientists say that for time travel a person would need to travel the speed of light—186,000 miles per <u>second</u>!

Dear Randy,

Time travel is an exciting idea. Wouldn't you like to meet Daniel Boone or Clara Barton or Jesus? Scientists say that to go back in time, a person would need to travel the speed of light—186,000 miles per *second*. Definitely too fast for turtles!

Nobody is totally happy with his past, but the way to make things better is not by going back. "Forgetting what is behind . . . I press on toward the goal." (Philippians 3:13–14, NIV) The only time we have to live in, Randy, is now. We can't go back to yesterday or zap ourselves forward to tomorrow. Today's all we need! If you want to make your life better, that's the very place to start. Change a habit, make a friend. Study, sing, laugh and love. You can do it all without ever traveling further than where you are right this very minute!

WALLY

Dear Wally,

I'm having this problem with two of my friends. They don't like each other very well. And at lunch I don't know who to sit with. I'm afraid they'll get mad at me if I sit with the other. What should I do?

Lindsay

Dear Lindsay,

Did you ever play tug-of-war, where two teams pull on a rope until one is dragged across a line or into a mud puddle? It can be lots of fun—as long as you're not the rope.

Why don't your two friends like each other? Could it be they're jealous of you? Try to think of activities that the three of you can do together—go skating or window shopping, work on a science project or be on a kickball team. Let each one of them know that she is important to you, but that you want other friends too. And you shouldn't have to "choose" which one to sit with in the cafeteria. All of you can sit together!

WALLY

Dear Wally,

    I have to go to my dad's house because my mom and dad are divorced. My dad screams and yells at me. And the court will not let me tell them whether I want to go or not. I don't want to go! Please help me!

Hettie

Divorce happens to over 1 million kids every year.

Dear Hettie,

We turtles are, by nature, quiet creatures. But human beings make all sorts of noise! They squeal at scary movies and cheer at basketball games and giggle at slumber parties. And sometimes they yell at each other.

People yell for all kinds of reasons. Sometimes they get mad easily, or they think they have to yell if they want people to listen to them. Often it's just a way of letting their unhappiness out. And all too often that unhappiness—and the yelling—get dumped on someone close at hand. Maybe that's what your folks are doing. Even though it may not seem like it to you, I'm sure they love you.

Who else have you talked to about this problem? Your father? How about your grandmother? What about your mother? Does your family know how upset you are? Maybe you can talk to a school counselor or social worker about ways you and your family can have some fun times together.

In the meantime, look for good things. And be sure your own words are "a gentle answer" that will "turn away wrath" and not "stir up anger" (Proverbs 15:1, NIV).

WALLY

Dear Wally,

My uncle does drugs. I am afraid that he will die. I can't sleep at night. He yells at me when I tell him to stop. I cry a lot. I am so scared. He says that we do not need him. But we do. What should I do?

Matthew

Dear Matthew,

It's really sad when you see someone you love making wrong choices for his life. And doing drugs is really a wrong choice! Your uncle probably doesn't like himself very much right now, and that's why he says nobody needs him. Show him that *you* need him—ask him to help you with your homework, play a game with you, or even go on a bike ride. Tell your uncle how much you love him, how much you'd like to see him get the special help he needs to kick drugs. You might want to talk this over with an adult who knows and loves your uncle too.

It's important for you to remember, though, that he is responsible for his own choices. Only *he* can take the steps to change his life. You can pray for him and encourage him, but only he can do it. Remind your uncle that he can do *anything* "with the help of Christ who gives me the strength and power" (Philippians 4:13, TLB).

I'm glad your uncle has someone like you—someone who loves him so much.

"My uncle does drugs. He yells at me when I tell him to stop."

Dear Wally,

My dad is having some problems. He is in the hospital because he is depressed, and sometimes it's hard for me. I feel real tight inside. I feel like crying sometimes.

Rachel

Dear Rachel,

When someone you love is hurting, you feel sad, frustrated, helpless. And sometimes crying is the *right* thing to do, no matter how old you are. It can give you some relief from those feelings.

Maybe it will help to know what good places hospitals are. Your dad can get the best care there. He is surrounded by people especially trained in how to make him well. They know what to say and do, what medicine to give him. So even though you don't get to see him as often as you'd like, it is really a good thing that he can be where he is. It will help him get better faster!

Maybe there are some things *you* can do for your dad too. Send him lots of notes and cards. Why not draw him a picture, a happy sunshiny one? Or write him a silly riddle or poem to make him smile. If you get to visit him, take along something for the two of you to do. A pad for playing tic-tac-toe or a coloring book for sharing.

And you can pray. "Don't be weary in prayer; keep at it; watch for God's answers and remember to be thankful when they come" (Colossians 4:2, TLB). God understands what's going on, even if you don't. He loves your dad—and you. He's ready to help you both!

WALLY

Dear Wally,

I have a big problem. All the kids at school hate me and make fun of me. At P.E., none of the kids will let me play basketball so the teacher makes them let me play. And I don't like the feel of it. What should I do?

Krystal

FUN FACT

Bounce...bounce, whirrr, swish! Basketball has come a long way since 1891. That's the year James A. Naismith nailed two half-bushel peach baskets to posts and played the first game. Basketball was born! But one piece of equipment that was essential then is no longer needed today: a ladder. The peach baskets still had the bottoms in them, and every time someone made a basket a ladder had to be brought onto the court to retrieve the ball.

Dear Krystal,

Not everyone is going to like you. (A lot of people didn't even like Jesus!) It doesn't matter how sweet or smart you are, how fast you can run or how high you can jump. There will always be a few people who will—for some reason—choose not to like you. And they may even choose to say mean things to you. Focus on making a few good friends rather than in trying to get everyone to like you.

And don't let what other people say to you determine how you feel about yourself. If you like yourself, other people will like you more too. One way you can like yourself is by looking at all the things you *can* do instead of the things you can't. Maybe those great basketball players in your class are jealous of the high grades you get in math or the great pictures you draw in art or the wonderful way you can tell a story. That could be one reason they give you a hard time in P.E. Don't expect to be perfect, but work on improving the things you're weak in. How about practicing a few dozen free throws Saturday morning? Most of all, spend time with people who make you feel good about who you are— people who realize just how special you are!

WALLY

Dear Wally,
   I clean my room and it gets messy in a few days.
Can you help me?

                              Love,

                              Virginia

"Take a few minutes every day to keep your room the way you want it to be."

Dear Virginia,

Do you know how to swim? (It's one of *my* favorite activities!) Have you ever "treaded water"? You keep your arms and legs going and—miracle!—you won't sink, no matter how deep the water is. But if you just stand there. . . .

Keeping your room clean is like that too. You have to stay on top of things. Otherwise you find yourself buried under dirty jeans and wadded-up homework, puzzle pieces and doll clothes, forgotten plates of peanut butter and crackers . . . You get the picture.

So don't wait until you're sinking under clutter and dust! Take a few minutes every day to keep your room the way you want it to be. Here's some hints that will help:

1. Hang up your clothes as soon as you take them off. Sure, it seems like a bother. And you're in a hurry, right? But you'll be surprised at how little time this takes—and what a difference it will make in your room.

2. Have a special place in your room to put dirty clothes, maybe a laundry bag or old pillowcase. No more stinky socks or reeking T-shirts thrown everywhere—just whisk them into your dirty clothes bag.

3. Have a place for everything. If you don't already have shelves, maybe you could get some. Plastic crates or an old bookcase from the basement or even sturdy cardboard boxes make good storage. The important thing is to decide where everything goes. Then, when something is out of place, you can grin and say, "I know where you belong!"

"Everything should be done in a fitting and orderly way" (1 Corinthians 14:40, NIV). And that includes the way you keep your room!

WALLY

Dear Wally,

I am 11. Three years ago my parents got divorced. Daddy was arrested and sent to prison for molesting my older sister. Mom says she divorced him to protect me and my little sister (she's 7). He is out of prison now. I don't understand. He is so nice to us, but Mom says he hasn't really changed. My little sister and me don't get to visit Daddy overnight.

This year I go to junior high, and Mom is letting me come home on the bus and stay without a baby-sitter till she gets home from work. Once I saw Daddy drive by. I told Mom and she gave me a big speech about never ever letting him come in the house when she's not here. But I really love my daddy, and if he comes to the house here to visit me, I don't see what's wrong with it. I don't think he would hurt me. Can you tell me if this is OK? How can I get Mom to change her mind? Thank you.

J. J.

REMEMBER:
No one has the right to touch you in a way that makes you feel uncomfortable. Nobody. The law protects children from that kind of abuse.

Dear J.J.,

Have you ever played with dominos? Sometimes I like to set them up in long rows, almost touching, then push the first one and watch them all fall over. Things in life are like that, too. One thing leads to another. Since your father served time in prison, there was hard proof that he had done something very wrong to your sister. Remember—no one has the right to touch you in a way that makes you feel uncomfortable. Nobody. Not even your father. The law protects children from that kind of abuse.

Your mother is trusting you to stay by yourself after school until she comes home. Good for you! That's a big responsibility, so please don't let your father come into the house while you are home alone. That would be deliberately disobeying your mother—and that's wrong. Also, you could get your father in serious trouble by letting him do something the courts have said he is not allowed to do.

No one is asking you not to love your father. It's only natural to love both parents. And remember this: Just because you're not close to your father now doesn't mean that someday you can't be.

Talk to someone about how you feel—a favorite teacher at school, a counselor, your pastor.

God has promised, "I am with you and will watch over you...I will not leave you" (Genesis 28:15, NIV). So even though you're confused, know that God is there with you. Always!

WALLY

Dear Wally,

I've got this problem. I was peeking in the Christmas gifts when I was not supposed to. And now I don't want Christmas because I did something wrong. Can you help me get the Christmas spirit back?

Lawrence

Dear Lawrence,

What you're feeling is guilt. You did something wrong and now you're sorry. You want everything to be like it was before, when you didn't know what your gifts were, when you were excited about Christmas. Well, Lawrence, it doesn't work that way. You *do* know what your gifts are; you peeked. Things can never be quite like they were.

But that doesn't mean you can't enjoy Christmas or that you've lost the Christmas spirit! If you've asked God to forgive you, it's time to stop thinking about yourself—what you did and how you feel. It's time to begin thinking about others and the happiness you can bring them by your own gifts and love. Jesus said, "It is more blessed to give than to receive" (Acts 20:35, NIV). So start *giving*—a helping hand with Christmas baking, an hour shoveling the walk, an afternoon of baby-sitting. Before you know it, you'll have that tingly "can't-wait-till-Christmas" feeling back again.

And next year, don't peek!

WALLY

Dear Wally,

I've got this terrible problem. I can barely find time to read my Bible. Pleeeeeaaaase tell me how I can find more time to read God's Word.

Lurlene

Dear Lurlene,

It's tough to find the time to do everything. In fact, it's impossible! That's why you have to choose what's most important and *make* time for those things. Nothing is more important than getting to know God better. And one of the best ways to do that is by reading your Bible. God's word is "...a lamp to my feet and a light for my path" (Psalm 119:105, NIV).

But how can you work it into your already full schedule? Try this: Set aside a certain time each day to read. Maybe it will be first thing in the morning, before you go to sleep at night, or when you come home from school. Try to read at the same time every day. Soon spending time with God's amazing word will be a regular part of your schedule—just like brushing your teeth or saying your prayers. And if you slip up and don't read for a day or two, don't give up! Begin again and try even harder!

WALLY

INDEX TO BIBLE REFERENCES

INDEX TO TOPICS IN LETTERS